Para Carla y Cristina porque sin ellas no tendría tantas historias de animales que contar.
Para Robbie, Lydia Gloria, Pablo, Griselda y Andrés.
Para Lucian y Julián.
Disfrútenlo.

Published by Campanita Books, an imprint of Editorial Campana

For information regarding permission, write to
Campanita Books
Attention: Permissions
19 W. 85th Street, Suite A, New York, NY 10024
or by e-mail, write to campanita@editorialcampana.com.
www.editorialcampana.com

Library of Congress Cataloging-in-Publication Data

Picayo, Mario
A very smart cat = Una gata muy inteligente / written by Mario Picayo ; illustrated by Yolanda Fundora. -- 1st ed.
p. cm.
Summary: A very intelligent cat shows off her many extraordinary talents and goes on a surprising adventure. Inspired by a true story.
ISBN-13: 978-1-934370-00-1 (hardcover)
ISBN-10: 1-934370-00-2 (hardcover)
[1. Cats--Fiction. 2. Pets--Fiction. 3. Spanish language materials--Bilingual.]
I. Fundora, Yolanda V., ill. II. Title. III. Title: Gata muy inteligente.
PZ73.K437 2007
[E]--dc22

2007031300

First Edition, September 2008
Second Printing, June 2009

Book & cover design by Yolanda V. Fundora

Printed in the United States of America

9 8 7 6 5 4 3 2

A Very Smart Cat

Una gata muy inteligente

Written by / Escrito por

Mario Picayo

Illustrated by / Ilustrado por

Yolanda Fundora

campanita
BOOKS
NEW YORK

WELCOME

Can you please take my cat?
¿Me harías el favor de llevarte mi gata?

She never leaves the dining room table.
Nunca se baja de la mesa del comedor.

She sleeps in the fruit basket.
Se duerme en la cesta de las frutas.

If I leave food on the table, she eats it.
Si dejo comida en la mesa, se la come.
BIG YUM CHOCOLICIOUS!
Tasty Lunch Treat
ZANY ZING
Citrus

If I leave a
drink,
she drinks it—
including my
coffee.

Si dejo
algo de beber,
se lo toma.
También se bebe
mi café.

If I leave a magazine, she reads it and cuts out her favorite pictures.

Si dejo una revista, se la lee, y recorta las fotos que más le gustan.

11:23
ZANY ZING
Citrus Burst
Hot Spots
WIZ WIRELESS
This bill is PAST DUE

ZANYZING
mewow!
joop
K
ZANYZING
The KoolTones
World Tour

Si dejo el teléfono, hace llamadas de larga distancia (si vieras mi cuenta...)

If I leave the phone, she makes long-distance calls. (You should see the bills!)

If I leave my camera, she takes pictures. Lots of them.

Si dejo mi cámara, toma fotografías. Muchas, muchas fotografías.

If I leave a pen, she draws all over.
Si dejo mi pluma, lo dibuja todo.

If I leave the TV remote control, she changes the channel.
Si dejo el control remoto del televisor cambia de canal.
ZANY ZING
NEW
PAST DUE

If I leave my wallet
on the table,
she orders take-out.
Japanese food seems
to be her favorite.

But it gets
worse.

Si dejo mi billetera
en la mesa, pide
comida afuera.
La comida japonesa parece
ser su favorita.

Pero se pone
peor la cosa.

Dream
夢の庭
Kooky
Cola
ZANY
ZING
Citrus
Burst

If I leave my harmonica
on the table, she'll play
all night long!
Do you know how hard
it is to take a harmonica
away from a cat?

Si dejo mi filarmónica
en la mesa, la toca toda
la noche.
¿Tú sabes lo difícil
que es quitarle una
filarmónica a una gata?

If I leave my hat, she'll wear it. Same thing with my gloves.
Si dejo mi gorro, se lo pone. Y hace lo mismo con mis guantes.
Dream Garden SUSHI
夢の庭、
Kooky Cola

If I leave the house keys on the table, she locks me out!

Si dejo las llaves encima de la mesa, ¡me deja afuera!

So please take her!
Así que, por favor, ¡llévatela!
ADS (for real people)
FEED STORES
Boarding
Lessons
Training
Nutrena Feed
Topsoil
GREEN HERON FARM
WOODSTOCK, NY
GREEN HERON FARM, INC.
(845) 246-9427
www.greenheronfarm.com
Ray Cullen
Roberta Jackson
CATS TO GO
Help us stop the suffering!
animalkind
Adopt a cat from us!
Donate today & save a stray.
721 Warren St • Hudson NY 12534
518-822-8643
www.animalkind.info
FREE
Beautiful cat looking for a good loving family.
Well trained.
Does not require much attention.
Entertains herself easily.
VERY SMART!
518-731-CATS (2287)
GRATIS
Hermosa gata a familia cariñosa.
Bien entrenada.
Requiere de poca atención.
Se entretiene sola.
¡MUY INTELIGENTE!
ss from Bill's Garage
You will be...
Sawyer
CHEVROLET
SAWYER-16
Larry Siracusano
President
sawyerchevy.com
sawyerchevy.com
RTE. 9W • CATSKILL
518-943-1007
CARS AND TRUCKS
STORES / TIENDAS
HOOD & COMPANY
Kitchen, Bath and Home Essentials
VISIT OUR STORE AT 432 MAIN STREET, CATSKILL OR SHOP ONLINE AT WWW.HOODANDCOMPANY.COM
Store Hours
Mon, Wed, Thurs 10-8 pm, Fri & Sat 10-9 pm
Sunday 10-6 pm Closed Tuesday
Paint-A-Story
2nd & 4th Saturdays
at
Imagine That
A paint your own pottery studio
396 Main Street, Catskill, NY
tel. 518-719-1920
imaginethatceramics.com
Black Horse Farms
10094 US Route 9W
Athens, NY 12015
518-943-9324
www.BlackHorseFarms.com
Open 9am–6pm Daily (including Sunday)
Greenhouses, Farm Fresh Produce, Gourmet Foods, Homemade Baked Goods & Gifts
Stop by and see all that we have to offer
We're located just 6 miles north of Catskill, NY
ANIMAL CARE
SAUGERTIES ANIMAL HOSPITAL
Howard Rothstein, D.M.V.
Leslie A. Jacson, D.M.V.
Beth Cohen, D.M.V.
(845) 246-6150
163 Ulster Avenue
Saugerties, NY 12477
Office Hours By Appointment
REAL GOOD FOOD
Miss Lucy's KITCHEN
Restaurant * Bar
Seasonal Market Menu
Lunch * Dinner
Weekend Brunch
Open Daily
We Serve Only Local, Pasture-raised Meat, Dairy And Wild Fish.
Catering Available
90 Partition Street Saugerties NY
(845) 246-9240
CREATIVE MINDS
Campanita Books is looking for talented children book authors to pub
Send us your manuscript! Visit
www.editorialcampana.com or
write to: info@editorialcampana
attn: Alicia, Andy or McKinley (your
Join the LART famil
of artists and writers
Unase a la familia d
artistas y escritores de L
Visit us/Visitanos:
www.lartny.org
LART
LATINO ARTISTS ROUND TABLE
FARM EQUIPMENT
ANIMAL CARE
RHINEBECK EQUINE, L.L.P.
Nina Deibel, D.M.V.
26 Losee Lane
Rhinebeck, NY 12572
(845) 876-7085 • Fax (845) 876-8611
www.rhinebeckequine.com
Cell (845) 389-0200
nina@rhinebeckequine.com
BUSINESS OPPORTUNITY
Barber Shop-Very successful
Owner retiring. Located right on Main Street, established clientele.
Call for appointment: 262-5678

Oh! Never mind. She finally went out.

¡Ah! Olvídate. Finalmente se fue.

LOS GATOS
"ALL CATS ARE CREATED EQUAL"
NORTH AMERICAN TOUR
FARM BUREAU
GOT FOOD? THANK A FARMER
NEW YORK
LOS GATOS
THE EMPIRE STATE
DON'T
FIX ME!
NEW YORK
PFC 1985
THE EMPIRE STATE

I left my backpack
on the table.
My phone, my camera, my
wallet, my gloves,
my hat, my harmonica, and
my TRUCK KEYS
were in it!

Dejé mi mochila en la mesa.
¡Mi teléfono, mi cámara,
mi billetera, mis guantes, mi
gorro, mi filarmónica y las
LLAVES DE MI CAMIONETA
estaban dentro!

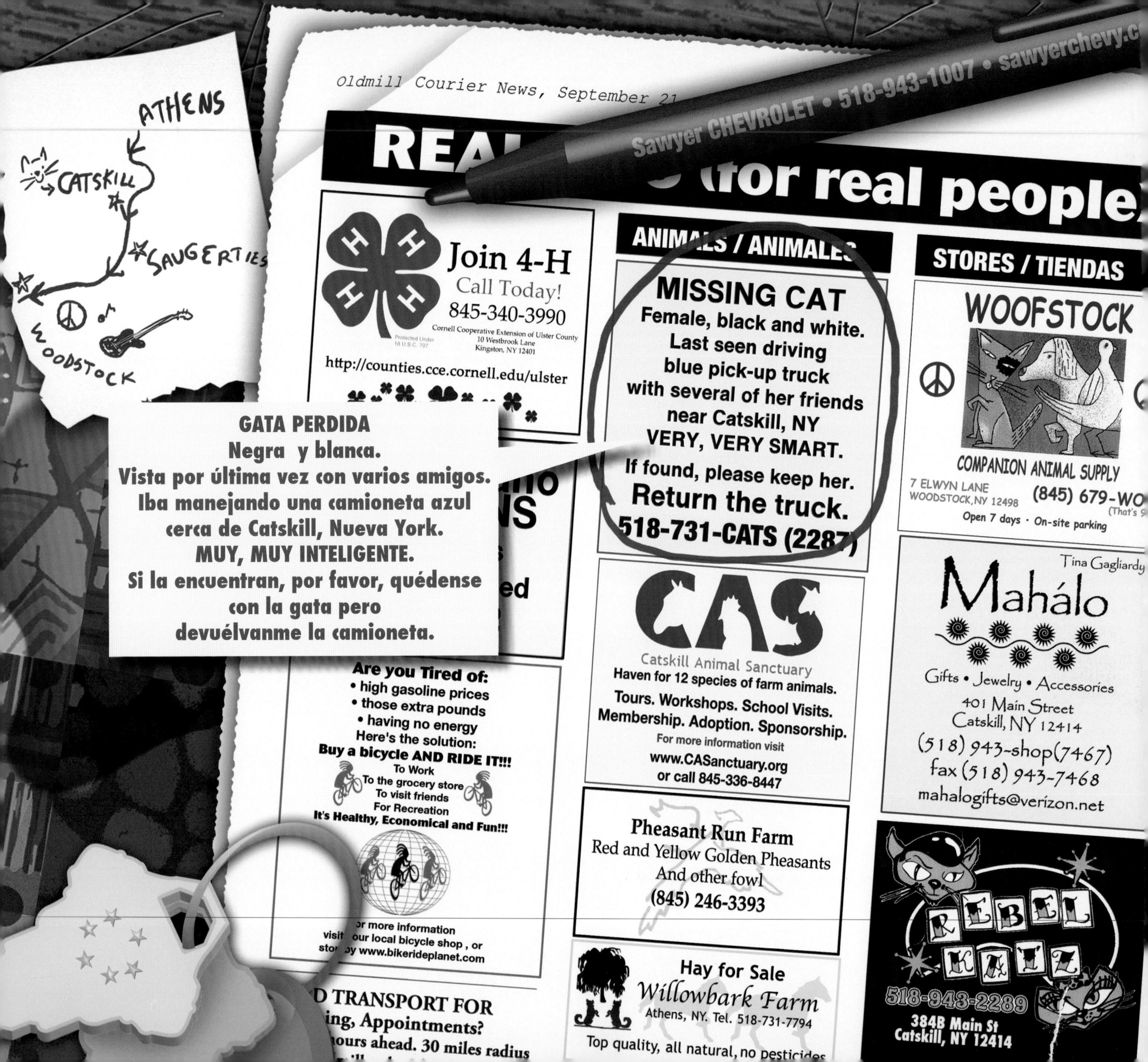

ATHENS
CATSKILL
SAUGERTIES
WOODSTOCK
Oldmill Courier News, September 21
Sawyer CHEVROLET • 518-943-1007 • sawyerchevy.c
REAL
(for real people
Join 4-H
Call Today!
845-340-3990
Cornell Cooperative Extension of Ulster County
10 Westbrook Lane
Kingston, NY 12401
http://counties.cce.cornell.edu/ulster
GATA PERDIDA
Negra y blanca.
Vista por última vez con varios amigos.
Iba manejando una camioneta azul
cerca de Catskill, Nueva York.
MUY, MUY INTELIGENTE.
Si la encuentran, por favor, quédense
con la gata pero
devuélvanme la camioneta.
ANIMALES / ANIMALES
MISSING CAT
Female, black and white.
Last seen driving
blue pick-up truck
with several of her friends
near Catskill, NY
VERY, VERY SMART.
If found, please keep her.
Return the truck.
518-731-CATS (2287)
STORES / TIENDAS
WOOFSTOCK
COMPANION ANIMAL SUPPLY
7 ELWYN LANE
WOODSTOCK, NY 12498
(845) 679-WO
Open 7 days · On-site parking
Are you Tired of:
• high gasoline prices
• those extra pounds
• having no energy
Here's the solution:
Buy a bicycle AND RIDE IT!!!
To Work
To the grocery store
To visit friends
For Recreation
It's Healthy, Economical and Fun!!!
or more information
visit our local bicycle shop , or
store by www.bikerideplanet.com
CAS
Catskill Animal Sanctuary
Haven for 12 species of farm animals.
Tours. Workshops. School Visits.
Membership. Adoption. Sponsorship.
For more information visit
www.CASanctuary.org
or call 845-336-8447
Tina Gagliardy
Mahálo
Gifts • Jewelry • Accessories
401 Main Street
Catskill, NY 12414
(518) 943-shop(7467)
fax (518) 943-7468
mahalogifts@verizon.net
Pheasant Run Farm
Red and Yellow Golden Pheasants
And other fowl
(845) 246-3393
Hay for Sale
Willowbark Farm
Athens, NY. Tel. 518-731-7794
Top quality, all natural, no pesticides
REBEL KATZ
518-943-2289
384B Main St
Catskill, NY 12414
D TRANSPORT FOR
ing, Appointments?
hours ahead. 30 miles radius

Note from the author

Like so many other books, this one was inspired by a true story.

My daughter Cristina and her husband Andy (and their children Lucian and Julian) live on a farm in upstate New York where, together with my wife, Carla, they rescue abused, injured, and orphaned animals of all kinds. One of the rescues was a cat that they were told was an "outside" kitty. Well, that cat discovered "inside" life and never wanted to put another paw in the outside world again. Cristina puts her out, and she walks right back in through the dog's door. She seldom leaves the dining-room table, which drives everybody a bit crazy. One night Cristina started complaining to me about this cat not leaving the table, and how she eats her lunch and drinks her coffee, and I added "and reads your newspaper," and from there on, the images of this kitty doing all kinds of mischievous things from her "dining-room table kingdom" just kept popping into my head.

My son Pablo contributed with a couple of "if I leave it on the table" items too. So I need to thank Cristina for giving me the idea for the story and Pablo for his contributions.

Photographs of the actual farm, truck, and of the real dining-room-table cat inspired the illustrations of the farm, the truck, and the cat.

The license plate on the truck at the end of the story reads "LOS GATOS", which means "THE CATS". That is really the license plate on our truck!

And last: The cat is still with Cristina and Andy (and Lucian and Julian), and they love her a lot, even if sometimes they wish that she would let them eat in peace and go play outside with the other cats, dogs, donkeys, horses, peacocks, guinea hens, rabbits, sheep, goats, and chickens that call the farm home.

Nota del autor

Al igual que muchos otros libros, éste se basa en una historia real.

Mi hija, Cristina, y su esposo, Andy, (y sus hijos Lucian y Julián) viven en una finca en upstate Nueva York, donde con mi esposa, Carla, rescatan animales maltratados y abandonados. Uno de estos animales rescatados es la gata de esta historia. A ellos les dijeron que era una gatita acostumbrada a vivir afuera. Pero resulta que la gata descubrió lo que es la vida "adentro" y nunca más puso una pezuña fuera. Cristina la saca y la gata logra entrar usando la puerta de los perros. Y es cierto que rara vez se baja de la mesa del comedor, y que vuelve a todo el mundo un poco loco. Una noche, Cristina comenzó a quejarse conmigo de la gata, me dijo que nunca salía del comedor ni abandonaba la mesa, y me contó cómo se comía su almuerzo y se bebía su café y entonces agregué: "y lee tu periódico". A partir de entonces, la imagen de esta gata haciendo todo tipo de travesuras en su reino de la mesa del comedor se quedó dándome vueltas y más vueltas en la cabeza.

Mi hijo, Pablo, contribuyó también con un par de "y si dejo esto y esto otro en la mesa del comedor". Así que les agradezco a Cristina las ideas para esta historia y a Pablo todas sus contribuciones.

Las ilustraciones de la finca, de la camioneta y de la gata están inspiradas en fotografías de la finca real y de la gata verdadera.

Al final de la historia, se puede ver la placa de la camioneta que dice: LOS GATOS. ¡Esta es la placa de verdad!

Y finalmente: la gata todavía vive con Cristina y con Andy (y con Lucian y Julián). Ellos la quieren mucho, aún cuando desean que los deje comer en paz y que salga de vez en cuando a jugar un poquito con los otros gatos, perros, burros, caballos, pavo-reales, guineas, conejos, ovejas, cabras y gallinas que tienen por casa la finca.

About the author: MARIO PICAYO is a writer, visual artist, cultural promoter, and animal right activist. Mario has worked at various capacities for organizations such as the Smithsonian Institution, the U. S. Virgin Islands Department of Education, the Department of Fish and Wildlife, and Sesame Workshop (Sesame Street). He is the author of the best-selling children's book *A Caribbean Journey from A to Y (Read and Discover What Happened to the Z)*. Mario and his family share their life with over one hundred rescued domestic and farm animals. Half the proceeds from his readings featuring *A Very Smart Cat* are donated to animal rescue organizations.
Contact the author at: Mario@editorialcampana.com

Sobre el autor: MARIO PICAYO es escritor, artista visual, promotor cultural y activista por los derechos de los animales. Ha trabajado para distintas organizaciones como el Instituto Smithsoniano, el Departamento de Educación de las Islas Vírgenes de los EE.UU., el Departamento de Pesca y Vida Silvestre y Sesame Workshop (Plaza Sésamo). Es el autor del best-seller infantil, *A Caribbean Journey from A to Y (Read and Discover What Happened to the Z)*. Mario y su familia comparten la vida con más de un centenar de animales domésticos y de granja. Parte de los ingresos que recibe por sus lecturas de *Una gata muy inteligente* son donados a organizaciones de rescate de animales.
Para contactar al autor escriba a: Mario@editorialcampana.com

About the illustrator: YOLANDA V. FUNDORA has combined her fine-art career with illustration and product design, and currently licenses her textile designs to the quilting industry. She has written two books with Barbara Campbell, *Holiday Quilts* and *Fuse It and Be Done*. She has also collaborated with botanical writer Marta McDowell on the book, *A Garden Alphabetized (for your viewing pleasure)*, which is based on her series of digital prints by the same name. *A Very Smart Cat* is the second children's book Yolanda has illustrated for Campanita.

Sobre la ilustradora: YOLANDA V. FUNDORA ha combinado su carrera en artes plásticas con la ilustración y el diseño de productos. Actualmente, sus diseños se venden en la industria textil. Fundora, junto a Barbara Campbell, ha publicado *Holiday Quilts* y *Fuse It and Be Done*. Su libro *A Garden Alphabetized: for your viewing pleasure (Jardín alfabetizado: para el placer visual)*, basado en la serie de impresiones digitales del mismo título, es el resultado del trabajo en colaboración con la escritora Marta McDowell. *Una gata muy inteligente* es el segundo libro para niños que Yolanda ha ilustrado para la colección Campanita.

About the translator: JACQUELINE HERRANZ BROOKS studied photography in Havana and became a writer by accident. She is the author of *Liquid Days* (TribalSong, 1997) and *Escenas para turistas* (Editorial Campana, 2003). Her work has been published in anthologies such as *Dream with No Name: Contemporary Fiction from Cuba* (Seven Stories Press, 1998), and *Aquí me tocó escribir: Antología de escritores latinos en Nueva York* (Trabe, 2006). She is currently finishing her M.A. in Spanish at City College and teaches at York College (CUNY). Among her interests are diaries as daily fiction, and photography.

Sobre la traductora: JACQUELINE HERRANZ BROOKS estudió fotografía en La Habana y se convirtió en escritora por accidente. Es autora de *Liquid Days* (Tribal Song, 1997) y de *Escenas para turistas* (Editorial Campana, 2003). Su trabajo ha sido incluido en diferentes antologías como *Dream with no name: Contemporary Fiction from Cuba* (Seven Stories Press, 1999) y *Aquí me tocó escribir: Antología de latinos en Nueva York* (Trabe, 2006). En la actualidad se encuentra terminando su maestría en City College y enseña en York College (CUNY). Entre sus intereses se encuentran los diarios como ficción cotidiana y la fotografía.

A few final words regarding cats

According to recent studies people and cats began their love affairs around 10,000 years ago in present-day Iran, Iraq, Israel, Lebanon, Syria, and Turkey. Nobody knows for sure how we came to be such good friends, since it all happened a long time ago, but it might have gone something like this: A female (perhaps pregnant) cat, either stranded or chased by a bigger animal, found refuge in some type of granary (that's where you store grain). Humans had just recently begun to farm and to store grains like wheat and barley for food. Rodents (mice and rats) enjoyed eating the farmers' grain, therefore farmers didn't like them too much. Imagine the farmers' surprise when they met the cat, a furry, cute, super hunter, who could keep rodents at bay. It was love at first sight, as they both realized what a great team they made. The farmer had no more rodents, the cat got a safe home and plenty of food. And that is how our friendship with cats may have begun. That first friendly cat had kittens, and people probably took them home to protect their grain, and so on and so forth. And as humans moved to new lands, the cats moved with them. So, as you can see, cats were not really tamed; they were wild animals that found a beneficial relationship with humans and decided to give it a try. They decided to domesticate themselves!

We love cats more than ever, and because we love them and because we have lived together for so long, we should respect them and be nice to them. If you have a cat, you should take good care of it and think of it as a friend.

Scientists say that the more than 600 million domestic cats living in the world today are descendants from just five original (or founder) cats. Wow! Many of these millions of cats have homes, but many others live in shelters where they wait to be adopted. Other cats have no home at all. Visit your local animal shelter to learn more about how to make the world a better place for all cats.

A few facts you may like to know about cats:

- There are approximately 88 million owned cats in the United States.*
- There are approximately 60 to 100 million not owned (feral, stray, alley) cats in the United States.**
- Nearly 34 percent of U.S. households (or 38.4 million) own at least one cat.*
- Eighteen percent of owned cats were adopted from an animal shelter.*
- Mexico has approximately 9 million cats.***

We do not want to close our book without sending a big thank-you to organizations like the ASPCA® (www.aspca.org), Catskill Animal Sanctuary (www.casanctuary.org), Best Friends (bestfriends.org), Animalkind (animalkind.org), and to the staff of shelters, sanctuaries, clinics, and hospitals. Thank you also to all caregivers, for your commitment and dedication to the well-being of not only cats, but of all living creatures needing medical asssistance, a home, a meal, or a hug.

*Sources/Fuentes: *2007–2008 National Pet Owners Survey. APPMA, American Pet Products Manufacturers Association. Website: www.appma.org. **Humane Society of the United States. Website: www.hsus.org. ***www.perros-purasangre.com.mx*

Algunas palabras finales sobre los gatos

Según estudios recientes, los seres humanos y los gatos comenzaron sus relaciones afectivas hace aproximadamente 10,000 años, en los países que en la actualidad se llaman: Irán, Irak, Israel, Líbano, Siria y Turquía. Precisamente porque esta relación comenzó hace mucho tiempo, nadie sabe a ciencia cierta cómo llegamos a ser tan buenos amigos, pero imagino que pudo haber sido más o menos así: Una gata (probablemente embarazada) abandonada a su suerte o quizás acosada por un animal mucho mayor que intentaba cazarla, se resguardó en un granero (el lugar donde se almacenan los cereales). Hacía relativamente poco que los seres humanos habían empezado a cultivar y a almacenar cereales, como el trigo y la cebada, para su alimentación. A los roedores les encantaban los cereales. Las ratas y ratones disfrutaban muchísimo comiendo trigo y cebada y es por eso que a los agricultores no les gustaban mucho los roedores. Imagínate la alegría de los agricultores de antaño al encontrarse con esta fierecita lanuda, muy graciosa, buena cazadora, que podía ahuyentar a los roedores. Fue, sencillamente, amor a primera vista. Ambos reconocieron qué tremendo equipo formarían juntos. Los agricultores no tendrían más roedores y los gatos tendrían un hogar para protegerse con suficiente comida.

Y así es como nuestra amistad con los gatos comenzó. Aquella primera gata amistosa tuvo sus gaticos y los agricultores vecinos probablemente se los fueron llevando a sus casas para proteger sus almacenes y despensas y esta historia se repitió muchas veces. Y cuando los humanos se comenzaron a mudar a otras tierras, los gatos se mudaron con ellos. Así que, como puedes ver, los gatos no fueron realmente domesticados; eran animales salvajes que encontraron beneficiosa su relación con los humanos y decidieron domesticarse ellos mismos.

Hoy día, queremos a los gatos más que nunca y porque los queremos y porque hemos vivido juntos por tanto tiempo, debemos respetarlos y ser buenos con ellos. Si tienes un gato, cuídalo mucho y tenlo en cuenta como se tiene a un amigo.

Existen más de 600 millones de gatos en el mundo. Los científicos dicen que todos ellos descienden de solamente cinco gatos iniciales (u originales). ¡Esto es extraordinario! Muchos, de entre esos millones de gatos, tienen hogares, pero muchísimos otros viven en refugios donde esperan para ser adoptados. Algunos no tienen ningún hogar.

Si quieres saber más sobre cómo hacer del mundo un mejor lugar para los gatos, visita el refugio para animales cerca de tu casa.

Algunos datos interesantes acerca de los gatos:

- Existen aproximadamente 88 millones de gatos con dueños en Los Estados Unidos.*
- Se estima que existen entre 60 y 100 millones de gatos sin dueños (asilvestrados, callejeros, realengos) en los Estados Unidos.**
- Casi 34 por ciento de los hogares en los Estados Unidos tienen al menos un gato.*
- El dieciocho por ciento de los gatos con dueños fueron adoptados de algún refugio para animales.*
- Existen aproximadamente 9 millones de gatos en México.***

No quisiéramos terminar este libro sin agradecerles a organizaciones como ASPCA® (www.aspca.org), Catskill Animal Sanctuary (www.casanctuary.org), Best Friends (bestfriends.org), Animalkind (animalkind.org), y a todos los y las trabajadoras de los refugios y santuarios, clínicas y hospitales. Muchas gracias también a todas las personas comprometidas y dedicadas no sólo con el bienestar de los gatos y gatas sino también con el de todas las criaturas vivientes que necesitan de un hogar, de comida, de atención médica y de cariño.